THE ABCs OF DISABILITIES

Written by **SEAN GOLD**   Illustrated by **ANNA & DANIEL CLARK**

Crippled by Culture, LLC
St. Louis, MO

Hi, I'm Sean!

Hi! My name is Sean, and I am the author of this book.

I was born with a disability, and lots of people — both kids and adults — ask me questions about what it's like. Maybe you have questions too.

So I wrote this book to answer some of those questions!

Perhaps you have a disability. Or maybe you don't, but you want to learn about them. Either way, this book is for you — from A to Z!

?

Where is Sean

There are three more illustrations of me as a child inside this book. See if you can find them all! The answers are at the back of the book.

A is for Accessibility

Some kids may speak, hear, see, or move one way. Others may speak, hear, see, or move another way. That's why **accessibility** is important, so as many kids as possible can easily enjoy the same places and activities. Kids with disabilities may need extra tools to do the tasks or another person to help out. But this way, everyone can take part in having fun!

B is for Bathroom

Some kids need help in the bathroom.

They may need help putting toothpaste on their toothbrush or using the toilet. Others may not be able to wash up or brush their hair on their own. Some disabled kids don't need any assistance at all — it depends on each person.

C is for Communicating

Communicating has two parts: talking and listening!

Kids can speak out loud or use sign language with their hands if they are deaf. They may use a communication board with pictures or a Talker that speaks out what they type. Kids can listen using their ears and eyes. They may use a hearing aid or a hearing dog.

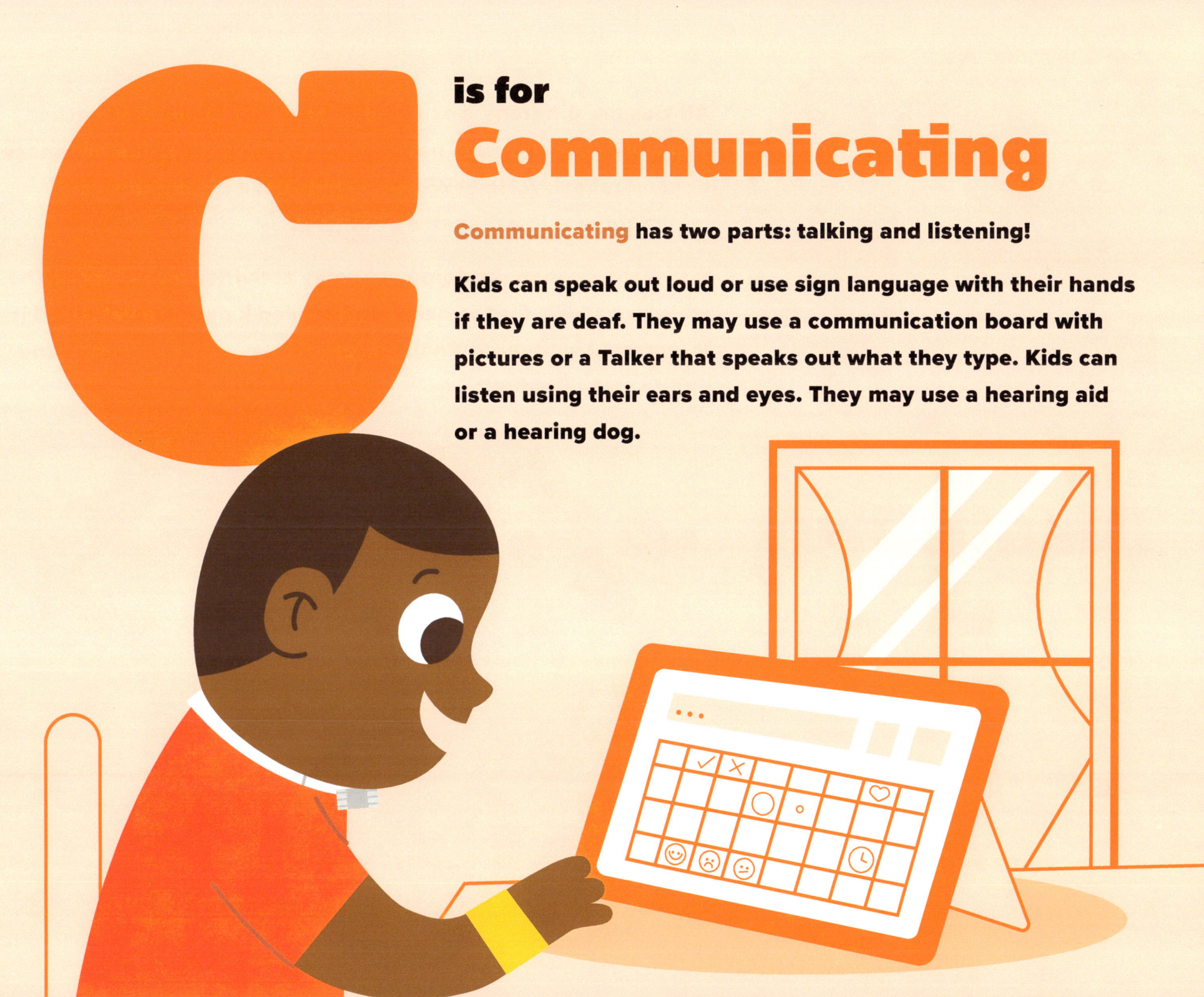

D is for Disability

All kids are different, and it's okay to notice their differences. You might notice if kids have a physical disability, like blindness or cerebral palsy. However, some kids have disabilities you might not see, like diabetes or autism.

A **disability** can make doing everyday activities a challenge. The world isn't built for the needs of disabled kids quite yet. Until it is, we must work hard finding creative ways to get things done and to make life fun!

E is for Eat

All kids eat, but there are so many different ways to do it!

Some kids can feed themselves. They may use a spoon and fork or maybe chopsticks. Some need an adult to help them eat. Some kids use a feeding tube. Water, nutritious formula, milk, juice, or blended-up food can go through the tube directly into their stomach.

G is for Glasses

Some kids wear glasses to help them see better. Without their glasses, the world may always look blurry. Maybe things only look blurry when they are far away or only when they are close up. Some kids may need to wear glasses only sometimes, but others may need to wear them all the time.

H is for Help

Do your friends ever need help? Ask and make sure, then do it! Lend a hand on the playground or share ideas about what books to check out at the library. Open the door or help out with homework. There are plenty of ways to lend a hand!

I is for Imagination

Blast off into space using your imagination!

If you're nondisabled, you might imagine flying a spaceship in a regular command chair. A disabled child might imagine flying their spaceship in a command *wheel*chair!

What about you? What do you imagine?

J is for Joy

Hurray for the feeling of joy! Some kids feel joy when they get good grades. Some feel joy when they do things on their own, like getting dressed or walking their dog. Some feel joy when they're in the park with their friends on a sunny day. Every kid deserves to feel happiness.

K is for **Kind**

Be kind to others. Notice what someone else is good at and tell them! Sit with someone new at lunch. Be kind to yourself too. Kindness can go a long way in making all kids feel happy, safe, and loved!

L is for Leader

A **leader** shows the way and inspires others to follow!

Sometimes you may want to follow, but other times, you may want to be the leader. Everyone deserves a turn to lead the way and share their great ideas. You do too!

M is for Moving

Let's get moving!

Some kids crawl, walk, or run. Some use walkers or wheelchairs. Some kids ride bikes or scooters. How do you get where you want to go?

N is for Normal

What does the word normal mean? It depends on who you are and what you're used to. Living without a disability can be normal for one child. Living with a disability can be normal for another child! Everyone has their own meaning of what is normal for them.

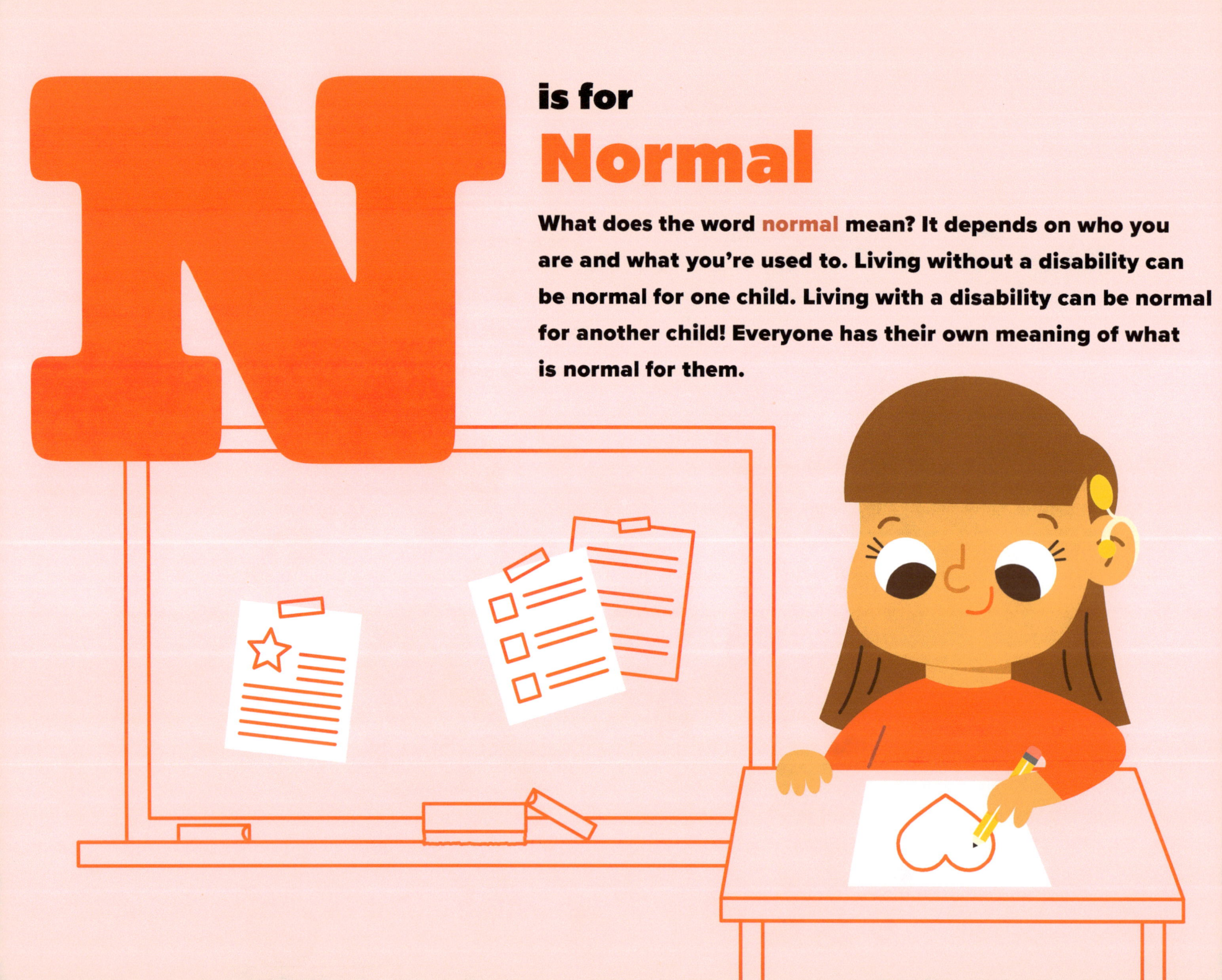

P is for Play

All kids love to play — whether it's running on the playground, using an iPad or computer, or acting silly with friends. When you play, find ways to include everyone!

is for Questions

Asking questions is a part of growing and learning. When you see someone with a disability, don't stare. You can say hello like you would to anyone else. And if you have a question, that's okay. Just be polite and get their permission to ask it first.

If you have a disability and someone asks if they can ask you a question, it's okay to stop and think about it. It's okay to say, "No, not right now," or to say, "Sure!"

R is for Reading

Are you enjoying reading this book? I hope so!

Kids can enjoy stories all kinds of ways: in physical books, e-books, or Braille books. Listening to audiobooks is another way to read too!

S is for Share

Sometimes it's nice to have something all to yourself, but sometimes it can feel good to share. Give someone else a chance to play with your toy, or ask a friend to play with you. Do your disabled friends play differently than you? Maybe you'll learn a new way to have fun!

T is for Therapy

Many kids need extra help or different kinds of help to do everyday tasks, whether it's moving, eating, or communicating. They might work with therapists, who help kids figure out what works for them. Therapy is important because it gives kids the help they need.

U is for Understand

It's important to **understand** other people besides ourselves. Of course, each of us are super special, but let's try to understand how others are feeling and thinking.

Understanding others will help us get along better, feel safer, and understand ourselves better too!

V is for Voice

What is important to you? Use your **voice** to share your beliefs and ideas. Speak up and communicate! Kids with disabilities can use their voices to communicate what they need, how they feel, or what they think. Your words are powerful. Share them with respect, care, and kindness.

W is for Work

Sometimes a disability can make doing something harder than it might be for someone without that disability. Maybe it is setting the table or picking up toys. Maybe it is doing physical therapy exercises or pushing the shopping cart at the supermarket. Kids with a disability may need more time and to **work** harder to do something.

X is for eXpert

Remember: No one knows what it feels like to be in your body better than you! Yes, you should always listen to your parents and doctors. But you'll know what is best for you. You are the expert on how you feel.

Y is for You

Yes, *you*, the reader!

I wrote this book, but you are the true star! Perhaps you have a disability. Or maybe you don't, but you are interested in learning about disabilities. That is so cool!

I hope you feel better about talking with other kids about disabilities now.

Z is for Zzzzz

What's one thing all children do, disabled or not? That's right, zzzzzzzz... they sleep!

Some kids use a humidifier when they sleep to help with their breathing. Some kids have a night-light, and others like to sleep in the dark. Some kids sleep in beds with padded side rails to keep them safe. But everyone sleeps!

Sleep well to get the rest you need to grow, and thank you for reading!

Conversation Starters

- Did you learn anything new in this book?
- Are there any drawings you wish you could add to this book? Why?
- Which was your favorite word in this book?
- What words would you add to this book? Why?
- Which was your favorite picture in this book?
- What do you want to know more about?

Where is Sean

Answers:

C is for Communicating

M is for Moving

Z is for Zzzzz

Dedicated to my grandmother and aunt. Forever resting in Heaven.

THE ABCS OF DISABILITIES
© 2024, Sean Gold

All rights reserved. This book or any portion thereof may not be reproduced or used in any manner whatsoever without the express written permission of the publisher except for the use of brief quotations in a book review.

To order copies in bulk, or for information about permission to reproduce selections from this book, please contact the author at authorseangold@gmail.com.

This book was made possible with support from the Regional Arts Commission.
Learn more at racstl.org.

This book was created with help from Editwright.
Visit editwright.com for more information.

Creative direction by Andrew Doty
Developmental editing by Susan Hughes
Copyediting by Allison Janicki
Book design and cover design by Anna and Daniel Clark
Proofreading by Karen L. Tucker
Published by Crippled by Culture, LLC

Typeset in Proxima Nova, Bemio, and Spade Round
First Printing: 2024

ISBNs
Hardcover 978-1-7368610-2-8
Paperback 978-1-7368610-4-2
eBook 978-1-7368610-3-5
Audiobook 978-1-7368610-5-9

Library of Congress Control Number
2024909982

BISAC
JUV039150 JUVENILE FICTION / Disabilities
JUV009010 JUVENILE FICTION / Concepts / Alphabet
FAM012000 FAMILY & RELATIONSHIPS / Children with Special Needs

Printed in the USA
CPSIA information can be obtained
at www.ICGtesting.com
LVHW071259210924

791652LV00005B/85